For C.M.S,
Best wishes always!

Da

Fe

They Might Be Poems

David H. Reinarz

Copyright © 2020 David H. Reinarz

All rights reserved.

DEDICATION

TO LYNNE:
WITH YOU
PREVIOUSLY UNIMAGINABLE JOY
PRESENTS ITSELF EVERY DAY

David H. Reinarz is the sole holder of the copyright for this book, "They Might Be Poems."

ISBN#: 9798616818560

Also by David H. Reinarz:

Exit Signs: A Collection of Short Stories
2018

Is That A Short Story In Your Pocket, Or Are You Just Happy To See Me?
A Bunch of Short Stories
2019

Table of Contents

ACKNOWLEDGMENTS

Thanks to Steve Langan, director of the 7 Doctors Project Writers Workshop for his support and inspiration. Thanks also to the numerous friends and family who have read and commented on these poems. Special thanks to Lynne Newville, Greg Chambers, Grace Davis, Teresa Eirenberg, Michelle Huber, Rick Spellman, Stephanie Plummer, and Steve Jordon for their work on critiquing the text.

AUTHOR'S NOTES

The poem, "Album Cover: Songs from the Country Western Café," was originally published in the Winter, 2017 edition of Plainsongs, Hastings College (NE) Press.

The poem, "Betray Al, Dinosaur, Sunset, Bicycle," was originally published in the Summer, 2018 edition of Plainsongs, Hastings College (NE) Press.

The ekphrastic poem, "Sanctuary," was inspired by the painting of the same name by Judith Anthony Johnston.

PREFACE

They might be poems.

If you are a literary critic or a creative writing instructor or a poet, you might think that calling this stuff poetry is just wrong. OK, sure.

Poetry in the 21st century is a varied and many splendored thing.

I'm suggesting that everybody just relax and try to enjoy the experience and not be too judgmental.

ALBUM COVER:
"SONGS FROM THE COUNTRY WESTERN CAFÉ"

Side A

1.The time I spent with you
is like the piece of gum
I just scraped off the sole of my boot
and tossed out the window of my truck
into the Texas night.

2.You broke my heart
like the last Ritz cracker
in the bottom of the waxed paper sleeve.

3.Sweet Jesus,
teach me how to make banana bread
from the shriveled up, stinky blackness
of my life.

4.I was drinking gin and vermouth
in a bar in Duluth,
I passed out in the booth
and broke my front tooth,
now everyone I meet
thinks I'm from OKRA-HOMA.

5.You served me road kill on a platter,
but I guess that doesn't matter
as long as you're happy to see me.

6. If I had drunk all the Kool-Aid
you gave me to drink,
I'd feel even worse than I do.

Side B
1.My dog likes lickin'
the skin on your fried chickin,
so I think I'm pickin' you.

2.Your kiss stays on my lips
like orange Cheetos powder.

3.Liver and onions, baby,
you know what I mean!

4.Lemon meringue pie
makes me think of the sky
filled with sunshine and clouds,
and I am so proud
to be an American!

5.If my daddy had taught his little girl to play tennis,
I wouldn't have missed you with that frying pan.

6. I want to be the corn dog
in the State Fair of your life.

7.Sorry I dozed off
just before you said you loved me,
but thanks for dinner, anyway.

Grounded

He had to ground himself before he kissed her.
I don't mean he had to steady himself,
plant his feet firmly on the ground,
although that would be an appropriate preparation
for what was about to happen.

He had to ground himself before he kissed her,
because sparks were going to fly.
He wasn't sure if the flow of energy
was coming from the sky
and channeling through her
or coming from the earth in some eruption via him.
Maybe it was both.
Maybe it was the concatenation of circumstances
that brought them together.
Maybe the power present
in the close proximity of their lips
was more than the cosmos could keep under control,
and it just burst out in an act of spontaneous combustion.

Whatever.
No one should be harmed.
He touched the lamp at the bedside.
The light flickered briefly then extinguished.
As he leaned in, a blue and gold finger of electricity
arced from her finger to the metal bed frame.

Their lips touched.
The cosmos sighed
then smiled.

David H. Reinarz

Moon June

The Jackal's teeth gleamed yellow white
in the dim light outside the bar.   moon

It was early for me to be drinking,   soon
and it was unseasonably hot
for a summer evening.   June

The way the Jackal looked at me,
like he was trying to dial in
some static-y frequency,   tune
it made me nervous, shaky,
a little dizzy.   swoon

I walked past him
into the dark, chillingly cool bar,   saloon
giving him a little sideways glance
as I passed him.
He had a tough guy smirk
on his face.   goon

I took a seat at the bar.
The bartender looked over at me
and raised an eyebrow.
I could see the thought bubble   balloon
over his head as he wondered,
"What's a nice girl like you
doing in a place like this?"   cartoon

"Dirty martini. Two olives.
Stirred, not shaken,"   spoon
I ordered.
The bartender had long hairy arms.   baboon
He smiled,
as he skewered the fruit
with a frilly cocktail pick.   festoon

The Jackal took the stool
beside me at the bar
And ordered a whiskey, neat.
He laid a twenty on the bar.
"And hers."   boon

Maybe he could tell
that the thing with the last guy
almost killed me,
that I was vulnerable,
that my thoughts and feelings
were scattered.   strewn

Here was a guy,
a random other guy,
to take what was left
of the other guy's kill.   impugn

"Drink up!" he said.
"Even when life's
not a day at the beach,   dune
we can drink."

"Drown my sorrows?"   monsoon
I laughed insincerely.

"Was I being too forward,   inopportune
buying your drink?" he asked.

"Not really."
We had just met,
but we knew each other well.
I was crying a little,
just enough to make my mascara run.   raccoon

I got up and headed for the bathroom.
Not the bathroom, the back door.
The Jackal followed my lead.
He kissed me
in the alley.
As he leaned into me,
I eased my blade   harpoon
between his fourth and fifth ribs
near the sternum.
The dark blood   maroon
trickled between my fingers
and dripped onto the bricks at his feet.

I sat at the bar
and ordered another martini.
The bartender gave me another look.

"We didn't really hit it off,'
I said.
"I had to cut him loose."   prune

I slammed down the martini.
The bartender eyed
the Jackal's twenty   doubloon
still lying on the bar
next to his empty whiskey glass.

"Keep the change," I said,
and stepped back out
into the hot summer night.   fortune

David H. Reinarz

Glance

"There are some people at whom one only has to glance for one's throat to tighten and one's eyes to fill with tears of emotion."
Drive Your Plow Over The Bones Of The Dead by Olga Tokarczuk

It was not the first glance.
The first glance of her,
sitting there,
dressed in black cashmere,
sipping the glass
of happy hour special cabernet sauvignon,
talking about renting a villa in Provence,
and inviting her friends and family
to share the sun of southern France,
resulted in a raised eyebrow of interest.

The throat tightening
and eyes filled with tears
came somewhat later,
a moment when I wasn't glancing at her.
No, not just glancing,
but looking deeply into her eyes,
not just beside her,
but reaching out and touching her hand
and having her wrap her fingers around mine.

It is years and years later,
and maybe my eyes don't fill with tears,
but I still get that tightness in the throat
and the catch in the breath
and the gooseflesh
whenever her hand welcomes mine.

David H. Reinarz

Sanctuary

I hang my head
on a hook
just outside the door.

I hang my head
on a hook
just outside the door
of my Sanctuary.

What good is a head, anyway?
A head?
A brain?
A mind?

A head is where the pain goes
to make itself known,
to make me aware
that it is always there.

The pain that distracts me
in the midst of conversation with a friend.
The pain that steals my appetite
when I want to eat.
The pain that taunts me with songs on the car radio
about sadness so inconsequential
that I laugh instead of cry.
The pain that tempts me with the desire to never wake up,
if only I could go to sleep.

What good is a head,
a head with ears
into which the pain can whisper,
urging me to resist it,
so that it can show me it is stronger?

I hang my head on a hook
just outside the door
of my Sanctuary.

I find the pain
deep in my gut,
and I invite it into my embrace.
I wrap it in the raiment of affection,
"my dear, sweet Pain."
I hold it close and crush it,
compressing it
into a smaller and smaller parcel
of all things irredeemably evil,
and then I slip with it
through the keyhole
into the realm of golden light,
and I float there
for a few moments
in my Sanctuary.

Inspired by
"Sanctuary"
A painting by Judith Anthony Johnston

Artists' Cooperative Fine Arts Gallery
Old Market
Omaha NE
April 23, 2017

Memory

Memory is very cruel, really.

It's not like it's this immutable cache
of   thoughts   and   feelings   and   faces   and   sensory
impressions
and totally accurate historical recountings
of all the events in one's life.

It's not like you can go there whenever you want
and re-experience the first time you saw her.

It's not like memory taps you gently on the shoulder
and whispers in your ear that it's her birthday
and here's a picture of what you did to surprise her
four years ago.

Memory fades
even if you are not in the midst of full blown dementia,
even if you are just going along,
living.
If you diligently fluff it up
with viewings of old pictures and videos
and readings of detailed journal entries,
and attendances at all the family reunions,
you can limit the damage,
but it fades anyway.

Even worse, memory changes.
You remember things that didn't really happen
the way you remember them,
or didn't happen at all,
or really happened to somebody else.
Our memory conflates things,
and you now think the neighbor's dog
bit the postman who brought you

the package sent by your grandma from California,
when what really happened was that the dog bit you
on the ass when you were playing football
with your friends in the front yard,
and your grandma was in Minnesota,
and it was your mom who was in California
when she was a teenager,
and the postman was an adult friend
you rode bicycles with in the Black Hills.

But you did really love that present.
It was a Hopalong Cassidy lunchbox set
that you got for Christmas the year you were seven.
And if you still had it now,
a collector would pay a stack of cash for it.

For a while, I thought I could depend
on other people who were there
or knew the people who were there
to fill in the gaps and sort out the confusions
or remind me of that time we did whatever it was
that we did.
But then I realized
that they have their own gaps and confusions
and misrememberings
and wishes that things had a gone a certain way,
and there isn't any one true source of knowledge
of the things that happened to me and around me.

But there is this beautiful woman
sitting next to me holding my hand and smiling,
and I think I remember that her birthday is coming soon.
And I think I remember
that the Hopalong Cassidy lunchbox
is in the basement of the house
where my parents used to live.
And I bet she would love to get that as a birthday present.

I could mail it to her.
It would be a great surprise
when the postman delivers it to her.

I can't remember if her neighbor has a dog.

David H. Reinarz

Overtaken

It was a day
when this particular person
had to get from this particular place
to that particular place
at a particular time.

I saw you in the distance.
I didn't know it was you,
not for sure,
but my brain had this intuitive moment of recognition:
your size and shape,
the angle of your back,
the pinched in narrowness of your shoulders,
the syncopated rhythm of your pedal stroke,
with the right leg doing slightly more work
than the left,
that you developed after the broken hip
you suffered
in that horrific crash two years ago.

Then my brain calculated
with its subconscious cycling math
that I could catch you
and say, "Hello,"
So I cranked it up to eleven.

As I started to close the gap,
you sat up
and took a long pull from your water bottle,
and I knew that red helmet
and that black and grey wool jersey
that you bought in Portland last year,
and I smiled.

I had almost overtaken you,
and I was thinking of the time
we organized that Doughnut Ride,
and nobody showed up but the two of us
because it was raining cats and dogs,
but we rode anyway,
and we each ate a dozen soggy doughnuts
and laughed a lot.

And then you turned off into the park,
and stood up and sprinted east toward downtown,
and I had to be in a particular place
at a particular time,
so I couldn't stand up and sprint east toward downtown,
and I was overtaken by a sense of loss
so profound
that all the strength drained from my legs,
instantaneously,
and all the air fled from my lungs,
instantaneously,
and, as I coasted to a stop
and dismounted
and leaned on my handlebars
and panted,
I anticipated tomorrow.
Tomorrow,
when I will overtake you.

Three Responses to a Funky Prompt:

Write a poem using the words "Sunset," "Betrayal," Bicycle," "Dinosaur."

Dinosaur betrayal bicycle sunset

He was a terrible lizard.
He admitted it,
bragged about it.
His "lizard brain" was overdeveloped
and highly influential on his behavior.   Dinosaur

His long forked tongue
flicked my earlobe
as he breathed hot moist lies into my ear.
Are they really lies
if I know they are lies
and he knows I know they are lies?
Or are they just things that are said
as a preamble to degradation?
Should I feel flattered or just complicit?   Betrayal

If I lie on my back and lift my legs
and move them in a reciprocal pattern,
I can hold him off for a while
while I think about what I really want.   Bicycle

Do I want the scales
and the cold-bloodedness
and the visceral energy
unrestrained by an evolved cerebral cortex?
Will I feel human in the morning?
His claw touches my lips.
"No more words."   Sunset

Sunset bicycle dinosaur betrayal

I like sunset.
The sky turns all kinds of pretty colors.
In the winter, it's not the coldest part of a day.
In summer, it's not the hottest part of a day.
It is better when there are some clouds
to reflect the light and mix it with shadows.

I like bicycles.
There is a pretty woman riding her bicycle with us.
We all left Ann's house,
and we are riding our bicycles across town to watch
fireworks.
I don't like fireworks.
They are loud, and they are a wasteful pointless display.
It is the Fourth of July,
and I like the pretty woman riding beside me on her
bicycle,
so I will make allowances.

We stop at a gas station
so one of the guys can go to the bathroom.
We haven't been riding that long,
but he has been drinking beer pretty much continuously
since five o'clock.
There is a green dinosaur in front of the gas station.
Two of the guys climb on the dinosaur,
and others take pictures of them with their phones.
The two guys on the dinosaur make humping motions
like they are having gay sex.
I don't normally object to this kind of thing,
but they are not gay,
and it's not really nice to make fun of people,
even if they are not around to know they are being made
fun of.

The pretty woman is standing next to me.
She says, "These are my friends, and they are morons.
What does that say about me?"
I smile.
I like the pretty woman.

We get to the place where we are going to watch the
fireworks.
It is sunset.
The sky is pink and gold and still a little blue.
I say, "This is better than fireworks,
all the colors without the noise and smoke
and stupid military music."
The pretty woman squeezes my hand and smiles.

It is dark now.
Rockets are exploding in the night sky.
I brought a blanket in my backpack.
The pretty woman is on the blanket with me.
We are commenting on each glittering burst,
which ones we like better and why,
the aesthetics of gunpowder and burning chemicals.
I like fireworks now.

The whole area is filled with acrid smoke.
All the friends have left us.
This is not really a betrayal,
because I wanted to be alone with the pretty woman.
Maybe it is a plot.
Maybe everyone wants us to like each other.
Maybe this is one of those times when people are nice.
Maybe life is not always filled with morons and stupid
meaningless displays.
The pretty woman squeezes my hand.
I say, "Do you want to go back?"
She says, "Not right away."
I smile and squeeze her hand.

Betray Al dinosaur sun set bicycle

It was inevitable
that I would betray Al.

Even though Al has been my friend
since before Nam
when we lived in caves
and hunted dinosaurs,
I wanted the woman.

He was not back before the sun set.
She was at my fire,
shaky from the cold,
trembling with the unknowing of his whereabouts.
I moved closer.

We did not know
that his bicycle had tumbled from the path
along the cliff,
and that raptors were picking at his bones
where his body rested, broken on the rocks.
We thought he might return
at any moment,
so we hurried.

Hey Jude, Don't Be Obscure!

"Hey, Jude!
Don't be obscure."
She said.
"Tell me how you really feel."
She said.
Was it a trick?
Could this be real?
Was this love.
or was it just another sad song
about an unemployed stone mason
and a pointlessly manipulative woman?
Still,
He hacked away at the granite
until her face was on every angel
on every church
in every town in the Midlands.
"Hey, Jude!
Don't be afraid."
She said.
"You want to get laid?
Don't worry about my old cuckold husband.
What?
Love? Sure."
Sex is no cure
for love.
Still,
he followed her,
stalking
over hill and dale
until there were holes in his stockings
and no good woman to darn them.
Darn her!
Still,

he gave her a box of rocks for her birthday,
each one carved and smoothed
into the face of one of their potential children.
"We would have beautiful children,
if I wasn't such a pill."
She said.
"Tell me what's moving
in that old rock upon your   shoulders, Jude."
Ah, rude feelings rear their ugly heads!
Still,
he let her take his heart.
Good riddance!
What good was a heart
when there was no revolutionary war
consummated by union.
Alone, he rocks in agedness
and carves a heart of stone to fill the hole in his chest.
Hey, Jude!
Be obscure, go ahead.
It's all cool, dude.

(With apologies to Thomas Hardy and the Beatles)

Intensity

Jhani put the picture down.
He flipped through some more photos in the box.
Photos from his dad's personal effects.
After the funeral.
Cleaning out the apartment.

He stopped.
He went back to that one picture.
He picked it up again.
There was something there. Something going on.
Something more than just people sitting around casually.

Why did his father keep this one?
He looked at it more closely,
trying to make out what it was
that drew him in and wouldn't let him go.
It was the only picture in the whole collection of artifacts
in which his mother appeared.

His parents were young here.
Probably before he was born.
Yes, the clothes and the style of the furniture.
It must have been in the 70's.
After the war.
Ski bumming around Colorado.
They were sitting on a couch.

They weren't looking at each other.

His father had turned to the right,
reaching out for the bottle of beer
on the lamp table with the moose on the shade
and the squirrel climbing up
the faux twisted tree branches toward the light.

Yes, Dad, intent on the beer.

While

His mother looked straight into the camera,
drilling whomever was behind the lens.
Her lips had just moved when the shutter clicked.
It wasn't a smile.
Her mouth, her whole body,
shouted into the photographic space,
"I will bite off your head. I will eat you.
But first, while your heart is still beating,
I will make love with you until I am satisfied."

The photographer must want this,
must want to not just make love to his mother,
must want to lose his head in her arms,
must want to be devoured by the force of her person.

Jhani felt a chill, goose flesh,
as he saw what his oblivious father was missing.

His father had thin strawberry blonde hair
that fell like a drizzling rain
onto the epaulets
of the drab army surplus store Eisenhower jacket.
There were faded blue jeans
and a toe sticking through a hole in his wool sock.

His mother was riveting,
with a face like Audrey Hepburn, only more feral.
Her dark hair was cut in a short bob.
She wore a tight black turtleneck sweater,
black ski pants, and hiking boots.
Her right hand held a glass of blood red wine,
her wrist at ease, the wine near spilling.

Jhani knew almost nothing of his father.
He couldn't remember his parents ever living together.
Even when he spent time with his father,
his father was someplace else, someplace far away,
someplace in another realm of consciousness.

"Jhani, Jhani, Khalil Gibrani," his father used to sing
as he drained another beer
and looked out through the apartment window
at the stars in the night sky.

His mother had read to him every night
when he was a boy
from The Prophet or Broken Wings
or some other Gibran tract.
What was the point of submitting a child
to this barrage of earnest romanticism?

Now, here she was again in his hand
in the wilderness of this ski lodge.
A glass of wine.
The winds of heaven.
A beautiful lie.

Why would he keep this picture?
He looked again at the intensity in her eyes.
How could you not want that?
Was it even possible to hold onto it
for more than a brief moment?

Jhani slipped the picture into the pocket of his jacket,
turned to his right, and reached for his beer.

David H. Reinarz

Sleep wraps itself

Sleep wraps itself
around my head.
I am restrained
by a vibrating, tingling halo of stars,
a cap of twinkling lights.
My body seems not fully connected to my mind,
arrested in some autonomic hibernatic cave,
yet it seems I should be getting up.
Sleep interrogates me seductively,
"Are you sure you want to wake?"
"Are you really capable of throwing off the bonds
that hold you in my realm?"
"You really want to remain in my embrace
a little longer, don't you?"
"What is it that you could do awake
that is better than your experience here?"
"Stay, look at this next dream!"
Somehow, my eye asks the clock for the time,
and some attachment to assignment
rebels against desire,
and then I am sitting on the edge of the bed,
and my feet are just touching the floor,
and my hand is pushing a forelock of hair off my
forehead,
and I waver for a second,
and another second,
and another.
What is it that I am supposed to do?
What might that next dream be?
Ah! Supposed to do.
Supposed.
How free am I?
Am I sufficiently powerful to disaggregate myself from
obligation?
How free am I?

Should I resist the siren's call of sleep?
Is freedom dependent on the ability to choose
and the will to pursue one's choices?
In the end,
I am a creature of obligation.
I am the one who gets up
and gets the thing done that needs to be done.
That is why I have an alarm clock.
That is why I wake up
before the alarm goes off.
I only flirt with sleep.
I am brushing my teeth,
now,
as the next dream lies
unrequited
among the rumpled sheets and blankets and pillows
of abandonment.

Moonrise

Because a full 59% of the Moon's surface is visible from Earth,
and my kitchen, on the main floor of my house faces east
and has an unobstructed line of sight to the horizon,
I have, with my own hands, punched a hole in that very wall
and inserted floor to ceiling custom glass French doors with transom.
I marvel that 59% of that satellite fills the doors with its cosmic self,
and that, by its light,
I can see the crumbs that have fallen from the toaster
and been kicked under the edge of the cabinets,
so I get the broom from the closet and sweep them up.

Because a full 59% of the Moon's surface is visible from the Earth,
and my bathroom is on the middle floor of my house
and its east wall faces in the direction of the Moon's rise,
I have, with my own hands, punched a hole in that very wall
and inserted a floor to ceiling custom crafted double hung window.
I marvel that 59% of a stone orb, 240,000 miles from the Earth,
with no natural incandescence,
can be a mirror for the Sun
and illuminate the page of the book
that I have taken from the bookcase at the top of the staircase
so that
I can recline in my bathtub
and read about the wreck of the Hesperus
without the aid of a lamp.

Because a full 59% of the Moon's surface is visible from
Earth,
    and my bedroom is on the top floor of my house,
    and, by the time I go to bed,
    the arc of the ascent of the moon has progressed to a
point
    that my windows are useless for viewing it,
    I have, with my own hands,
    punched four holes in the roof and inserted custom
skylights.
Though the Moon seems smaller than it did some hours
ago,
    59% of it is still the largest light in the galactic panorama.
    Most nights, I will lie on the floor on the Persian carpet
    that is spread out between the sofa and the bed
    and watch my moon as it travels from skylight to skylight
    until I fall asleep.

And as I sleep, I dream.
I dream about taking down the knick knack shelf
    that is over the washer and dryer in the garage,
    which is on the west side of my house,
    and punching a hole in the wall with my own hands
    and inserting a window,
    so the setting of the full 59% of the Moon's surface
    will be visible from that spot on the Earth.

Salt

You smelled her hair without shampoo,
without hairspray,
with just a dash of salt from playing in the ocean
that first time you were alone together.
So, you want that.
Always.

You smelled her skin without deodorant,
without perfume,
with just a pinch of salt from her perspiration
as you chased her across the sand
then tackled her,
and your nose ended up in the little hollow
where her collarbone meets her shoulder.
So, you want that.
Always.

You held your breath when you kissed her,
and her lipstick was washed off in the sea,
and your nose was next to hers
when she let go and exhaled,
and you breathed in her breath,
and there was just a hint of salt.
So, you want that.
Always.

If you see her on the street,
and it's been so many years later
that the polar ice caps have melted,
and the ocean has risen so there is no more beach,
and you call her name,
and she turns,
and there is a look of recognition in her eyes,
and you hold out your hand to her,
and she comes over to you, and you embrace,

and her hair smells like cigarettes,
and her skin smells like the cheap perfume
that was probably a gift from the last of a string
of faithless boyfriends,
and her breath smells like too many margaritas...

but you taste just a little salt along the edge of her lips.
That is what you want.
Always.

Desiccation in Four Parts

I.
Desiccation is something that happens
to you.
It's not the kind of thing you do
to yourself.

I mean, look at yourself!
You're a hollowed out shell,
a pile of dust in the corner,
fruit turned to leather.

Someone took your water.
You thought you were digging a well together,
tapping into an endless aquifer,
a resource to be shared.
The deeper you dug, the farther the water receded.

She licked the sweat from your body as you toiled.
She waved as she floated away on the great salt sea.
The dry hole is your grave.

II.
I found you in the desert.
You were lying on your back in the sand,
staring at the sun.

You appeared to be dried out,
desiccated.

I looked into your eyes.
The dream of oasis was
still alive in your mind.

I licked my lips and knelt to kiss you.

III.

An IV drips steadily into the vein in your arm. I check the flow rate and make a note in your chart.

The doctor palpates the flesh of your cheek. He makes me think of a frontier snake oil salesman. He tells you that the magic elixir we are pumping into your desiccated body will restore the elasticity to your skin, plump up your tissues, erase the wrinkles at the corners of your eyes.

Those eyes.

I hope he is a charlatan, a con-man, a hustler, this doctor, this man who preaches the plasticity of the human form, this purveyor of the fountain of youth. But maybe this treatment will work. I can see by the look in your eyes that you want it to work.

Those eyes.

I think that you shouldn't get to be young again. You should retire from being dangerously beautiful. You shouldn't be looking at me that way, your eyes anticipating my response.

Those eyes.

You remember what it is like to be filled with moisture. You remember the flow of fluids. You remember smoothness and firmness. You remember when you wielded the seductive power of physical beauty and charisma. You think you already have that back. I can see what you intend for me in your eyes.

Those eyes.

The world is filled with the desperate and the gullible. Perhaps I am desperate and gullible to believe that the world is a safer place without you in it. The doctor is gone now. I have the key to the locker where all the dangerous drugs are locked away. Your eyes look with a wild terror at the needle.

Those eyes.

IV.

This is not me.
Maybe you see a resemblance.
I used to be here.

I was a nymph,
an immature form of myself.
I am gone now, gone from what once infatuated me.

Desiccated in my absence,
a discarded exoskeleton that once encased me,
limited me, is only a former life.

I am juicy.
When my wings dry,
I will fly away.

David H. Reinarz

He fell from the sky

He fell from the sky
Onto the roof of her tent.

Luckily,
She had ordered the Super Duty Everest Base Camp
dome tent.
She didn't even know where Everest was,
Somewhere out there
Beyond the marshes of southern Chaldea.
Maybe she didn't need that much tent for the local
climate.
But why skimp?

He hadn't crushed her.
He had bounced off the arched nylon
And landed with a thud
Just outside her entry portal.

He was still smoldering,
Charred here and there,
Stubs of bone and gristle
Where his trapezius muscles had connected to…
Wings?

She did the math in her head,
Estimated his weight and surface area,
The constant for acceleration due to gravity,
Average air density above the Persian Gulf,
Terminal velocity,
Fire,
Equals distance traveled

Plummeting from Heaven,
Obviously.
Wings aflame

Heading straight to Hell,
Flung into space by Angry God
(God, could he be so angry!)
So angry he miscalculates the trajectory.
Flight interrupted by her tent.

That feckless man that lived with her
Had wandered off.
What a waste of human flesh!
More naming things to do.
"What's my name?" she yelled at his back.
"What's my name?"
"Wait Here," he said.

The desire to be Wait Here
Was not everlasting.
It had seeped from her soul long ago.

Recline in the tent.
Read a book.
Weave reed baskets for gathering food.
Catch some rays.
Repeat.

Now this Divine Creature falls from the sky.
Booted out for some perceived disobedience,
Some rebellion.
Burned, dewinged, but unbroken.
Disobedience stirred in her, Rebellion considered.

She turned him over.
She touched his face.
She dragged him into the tent.
She got water from the well.
She washed the carbon footprint from his skin.
She kissed his wounds.
He opened his eyes.

He took her in,
Took all of her in,
Everything outside and inside of her.
He smiled.
He seemed happy to see her.
She took him in.

She smiled.
"Are you hungry?" she asked.
"I have apples."

David H. Reinarz

The Fair

The ferret
went to the Fair at Styles.

He tasted the fare at
all the food stands
at the Fair at Styles.

He paid the fare at
the ticket booth
and rode all the rides
at the Fair at Styles.
He especially liked
The Tunnel of Love
which reminded him of his affair at
the burrow of his neighbor
back home in the Dakotas.
That pretty woman ferret
would have enjoyed
the Fair at Styles.

Some of the humans
at the Fair at Styles
had a rather laissez-faire attitude
about a ferret at the Fair.
As long as he had the coins
in his pockets
to pay the fares,
as long as he had the coins
in the pockets of the jeans he wore,
they didn't care.
(A naked penniless ferret
may not have fared so well
at the Fair at Styles.)
But, to be fair,

and one must be fair at all costs,
we all have costs.

So they didn't care.
Mostly.
Some did raise an eyebrow
at the flare at
the cuff of his jeans.
Memories of hippies in the Sixties
flared at the corners of their minds.
The memories of the working class
were a morass of pain
and unresolved offenses to sensibilities
even now
at the Fair at Styles.

But, when a ferret comes
to the Fair at Styles,
even a potentially ex-hippie ferret
with the flair to wear
jeans with a flare at the cuffs,
if he has coins in the pockets
of his jeans,
he will fare well at the Fair at Styles.

That night the fireworks display
at the Fair at Styles
shot multi-colored flares at the sky.
The ferret said farewell to the Fair.
He nestled in the pocket of the apron
of the widow woman who ran the funnel cake stand.
The swaying and bouncing of her old truck
rocked him to sleep
as she drove toward the seacoast.
It wasn't a burrow in the Dakotas,
but to be fair,
he could fare well here.

Six Odes

Ode to Bottled Water

Perrier.
Or was it Evian?
Maybe both.
The water drawn from an artesian well,
unpolluted,
always cold,
even in the heat of summer,
now available bottled,
in any port of convenience
anywhere in the world.

Perrier and Evian.
How could something so flavorless be so delicious?
How could something so uniquely refreshing become
ubiquitous?
She thought this.

Perrier and Evian.
Maybe she would name her kids,
if she had kids,
Perrier and Evian,
a girl and a boy.
Maybe she could have made those kids
with the guy she met
at Burning Man,
but her memories of him,
of that week in the desert
in which he was just one tree
in a forest of vague, dusty, unreliable humans,
were vague, dusty, unreliable.

Cold sparkling water.
She remembered that crystal clearly.

When you wanted to step out
of the maze of flesh and fur,
the haze of disinhibition and indiscretion,
someone would hand you a chill plastic bottle of
Perrier or Evian,
and it would shock you back into the realm of the
mundane.

The realm of the mundane.
She realized that she had stopped
mopping the floor in the men's bathroom
in the C-store on the highway where she worked.
The guy pumping gas a little while ago
had not been the guy from Burning Man
come to find her and tell her that she meant
something to him.
She had asked him.
He said he didn't know what the hell she was talking
about.
But, but, ...oh well...
She ran her forearm across her brow.
She drank from her chill plastic bottle of artesian well
water.
She felt Perrier and Evian move in her womb.
She heard the bell on the store door chime.
She parked her mop and hurried to the front.
Maybe this time it would be him.

Ode to a Gravestone

It was his last gasp,
his last stab,
his last quip,
his last detail,
that line of text
below the name and the dates of birth and death
on my father's gravestone.

"Get in, get out, don't leave too big a mess."

The little bit of worldly wisdom,
suggestive double entendre,
snarky before we knew what snark was,
but still true,
so true,
an aspirational meme for all humans,
for something which we rarely achieve.

I go to the cemetery
at least once a week
and sit beside his grave
and conjure up his wry smile and his knowing wink
and trace the words with my finger.

He did this a lot,
my father,
drop a little word bomb
into a conversation,
puncturing somebody's balloon of pontification
or hinting at something prurient
or making some mundane point more lyrical.

On the gravestone next to his
are my mother's name and dates
of birth and death,

some years before and after his,
and her line of timeless wisdom,
"Nobody likes a smartass"
seeks to deflect his heat seeking missile of wit.

In all the years
that I was around them,
close to them,
living with them,
I never really could tell for sure
if her criticism of him has just playful banter
or soul crushing animus
or if he took it with grace
or resented her attempts to censor him.
They were always well masked.

But it is undeniable
that he went out with a bang
and she with a whimper.

Ode to a Coffee Urn

There are no naked youths
cavorting on your flanks,
nor leaf fringed temples
recalling archaic days
when gods walked among us.
Yet, I give thanks this dawn
for your simple
brushed aluminum tank,
beauteous in ways subtle.

What's more,
you are not mere empty decoration,
for what's inside,
toasted seed of purple fruit
washed o'er with water pure
until it's hot and its murky potion
works as if by magic,
puts my day in motion.

Your percolating perks me up
though I was up
late last night,
perky,
chasing love,
panting
with breathless human passion,
then left for dead,
wrecked upon the shores of denouement,
only to awake, anon,
barely living,
plagued with burning forehead
and parch-ed tongue.

You are ever warm, my urn,

and earn my praise
through dutiful succor,
for I am a sucker for
fair attitude sans judgement,
thus thou art
a Friend of man,
and Art,
for coffee is beauty
and beauty is coffee,
and that is all ye on earth
ever need to know.

(With apologies to John Keats)

Ode For Wool

She pulled the wool under my eyes.

She kept it cool in the bedroom,
chilly really,
cellar temp.
Why? We weren't bottles of vintage pinot noir.

I was shivering,
not the best state for drifting off to sleep,
or drifting off to whatever
might happen in bed.

So, she got the extra blanket
(Northern Minnesota dead of winter grade)
from the top shelf in the closet,
unfurled it with a flick of her wrists,
and let it flop down upon me.

She straightened it out,
tucked me in,
and kissed me on the forehead.
Whether it was
that kiss
or the wool blanket
that did it
I will never know,
but I warmed.

David H. Reinarz

Ode to Blood

Ah, Blood!
Ye run cold.
Aye, ye run cold this day!

Ah, Blood!
Ye have coursed
through my body
in myriad homely channels,
feeding muscle and organ and bone,
stoking,
sustaining life,
fueling passion.

Ah, Blood!
I remember when
ye ran hot.
All was flush and heady
under yer feverish influence.
There was nought eschewed.
Seven sins were not near enough!

Ah, Blood!
Ye rose up in me
at the chance for taking.
The want had no cogent thought,
no care for consequence.

Ah, Blood!
All I saw was red.
Who could tell me, "No?"

Ah, Blood!
Now comes consequence--
What, Ho!--
to stake a virtuous judgement

against my desire.
En garde!

Ah, Blood!
I feel the rush of thee!

Ah, Blood!
Ye run cold this day.
I crave thee hot and bothered once more.
Yer taste is sweet and bitter
in my mouth,
a dissonant mixture.
I savor thee like honey,
yet spit thee out like bile.

Ah, Blood!
Ye run cold this day
as ye flow out of me
through numerous exsanguinous ports
opportunistically thrust upon me,
into me,
by consequential surprise.

Ah, Blood!
Your heat is chilled,
all thrill congealed
and turning into black.

Ah, Blood!
Ye run cold this day.
I float dimly
on a rising sea of thee.

Ah, Blood!
I knew thee well.
How is it ye were with me
so short a time?

Ode to Suitcases

His suitcase
sat on the desk
unzipped,
flipped open,
nearly spilling out its contents.
Her suitcase
was atop the dresser
anticipating,
waiting to be unstrapped.

This is how it was with them,
always,
trying to find the balance;
him striving to harness his need to be early;
she pushing the limit on what was fashionably late.

Yet, they traveled well together
and were well traveled.

The key elements were:
foldable,
stretchable,
casual,
durable,
comfortable,
hand washable,
and they were,
as was everything they packed.

David H. Reinarz

"The mellow autumn came, and with it came
The promised party, to enjoy its sweets.
The corn is cut, the manor full of game;
(Don Juan, by Lord Byron)

Byron's Daughter

"The mellow autumn came, and with it came…"
A partridge in the pear tree
outside the window,
the window of my suburban home.

How did a partridge get there?
They are country birds
pecking about in fields cut low by harvesting
hoping to glean a kernel or two of castoff grain.

Would this wandering bird even eat pears,
search them out in cityscape
having picked the brown farm dirt clean of dry corn?
He/she would be disappointed,
as it is ornamental, my pear.

My father planted it here
to give me something to look at,
to interrupt the expanse of turf
that extends mindlessly to the fence.
I love the white flowers in the spring,
and now
a plump grey and brown and white bird settles in
among the blaze of fall color.

I call it "mon Pere,"
my tree,

after my father
who so thoughtfully put it there,
the one who knew I needed an attraction,
a distraction,
a changing agent to break up the monotony
of staring all day at grass.

The sound is not a bang or a pop.
It is a harsh rush of air through a tiny enclosed space.
The partridge falls.
The branch on which it was sitting bobs
up and down
like the diving board at the community pool.
I can still see it above me as I sink,
a ribbon of blood furling out from my head.
"Mon Pere! Sauve moi!"
I can see the bird below my window,
a ribbon of blood furling out from its head.

The mad woman from next door creeps
into my yard,
the pellet gun slung over her shoulder
like a member of The Resistance.
She snatches up the partridge and bags it.
The pillowcase is embroidered with roses.
I know it.
I embroider to keep my hands busy
as I look out my window,
gifts for peoples' birthdays,
all the other holidays, too.

I turn and look out my other window.
She, the mad woman, is on the deck
connected to the back of the house,
just off the kitchen.
She is plucking.
The grey and brown and white feathers

go back into the pillowcase.
The brown and grey and white Cairn terrier
waits eagerly
for the disembowelment.
I close my eyes and turn away.
I look for my pear tree.
"Mon Pere! Sauve moi!"

The noise of the mad woman's autumn party
is loud enough that I can hear it,
even though my windows are closed.
The aromas of roast meat and root vegetables
pass through the walls as if they were not there.
Wine glasses clink,
guests drunk on the human liquor of harvest
laugh.

I close my eyes as I embroider roses
onto the hem of a pillowcase.
A ribbon of blood unfurls from a petal.

David H. Reinarz

Heaven Drunk

He was heaven drunk
He fell to his knees and gave his life to the Lord
He drank deeply from the grail of holy Grace
He was full of the Spirit
The hand of God rested on his head and blessed him
He saw the room in the mansion in the sky
where he would dwell forever
The world of struggling and suffering
decomposed into the dust of unconcern
He was bathed in the orb of golden light
Angels sang in celebration
His ex-wife admitted that he had been right all along
and she was really at fault for...for...everything
Young virgins, the daughters of other men, looked at
him with the eyes of pure desire
Choosing or asking were unnecessary for all things
were already in his hands
The sun and the moon and all the stars revolved
around him
His brothers handed him their mother's amber amulet
and their father's hunting knife
He felt the power of the Almighty surge through his
veins
He could act with impunity
He understood the pointless vanity of morals and
laws and social conventions
Judgement of him by others was no longer possible
The blood of the innocents was transubstantiated into
sustenance
Fear ran away and hid
He eschewed moderation
He floated in a sea of pure energy
Ecstasy was his new name
Darkness winked knowingly and gave him the thumbs
up

David H. Reinarz

__Tonight__

Tonight,
if you suck on my fingers,
they will taste like garlic.

Tonight,
if you kiss me,
my lips will taste like extra virgin olive oil
and white balsamic vinegar.

Tonight,
if your tongue can find the place
where the Montepulciano was spilled,
I will swoon.

David H. Reinarz

Pecan

A tiny bit of chopped pecan
stuck in the crevice
between incisors
only discovered
just now
when I ran my tongue over my teeth
as I was about to smile
at you
so I
in a state of embarrassment
sealed my lips
and you walked away
unseduced

David H. Reinarz

Desire

How do you take a sip of water from a flood?

Desire would destroy her,
if she allowed it.

Yes, little sips.
That was it.
And infrequently.

That's what she ought to have done.
Definitely.
That's what she ought to have done.

David H. Reinarz

Thin

Some of the cookies in the container weren't broken.
Some.
Less than half were whole.
But more than a couple.

They were so thin.
Brittle? Is that the word for them?
Thin and brittle?
Stacked in a container in which they could rattle.
Against each other.
As they are moved from place to place.

Mostly broken almond thins.
Pricey.
Imported from Belgium.

David H. Reinarz

<u>Sometimes</u>

Sometimes
when you are thirsty
you drink a lot of something
you don't even like

David H. Reinarz

Coffee

The coffee was cold and rejecting.
You could sense it as you picked up the cup
and stared at its vaguely oily surface.

It would be bitter about being left alone
on the bedside table
as you went to the bathroom.
Brushing your teeth would be viewed by coffee
as an attempt to wash its dark roastiness
from your mouth.

You had casually walked downstairs
to see what your husband was concocting for
breakfast and stayed.
Stayed and ate a cinnamon apple waffle
without liquid accompaniment.

You thought the coffee might still be warm
as you wandered back up to bed
with the Sunday Times under your arm.
Really?

The coffee wanted to be warm.
The coffee wanted to be cherished
before being approached by your lips.
That would only be right.
That would be respectful.
That would take into account the quality of
everyone's experience.

But that would entail going back downstairs,
and reheating it,
and, really,
the coffee already felt like yesterday's.

David H. Reinarz

Sex is dangerous

Sex is dangerous.
You're obsessed by the lust.
Your inhibitions are gone.
Your defenses are down.
You are in this moment entirely.

And then,
you float in the backwash of ecstasy.
You are as limp and powerless
as a leaf separated from its tree,
lying on the ground,
curling up in its disconnectedness.

The wolf is at the mouth of the cave.
It knows your scent.

You don't care.

David H. Reinarz

Press Firmly

I was filling out the form.
Three layers of paper.
White. Blue. Pink.

She put her hand on mine.
I stopped and looked up.
Our eyes met.

"If you want the tip of the pen
to have the proper effect,"
she said,
"press firmly."

"Always good advice,"
I said.

She smiled.

David H. Reinarz

Out of Place

You can't have the word "place"
Without the word "ought."
He thought.

"the specific portion of space
normally occupied by anything"

The thing is in its place.
It ought to be there.
If it is not there,
it is out of place.

If something is there that ought not to be there,
it is in the wrong place.
It is out of place.
It is out of its own space.
It is in something else's space.

Maybe the thing out of place,
in the wrong place,
that ought not to be there,
is a person,
is an interloper.

Interloper: "a person who becomes involved in a
place or situation where they are not wanted or are
considered not to belong"

He thought it was an interloper.
She thought it was a breath of fresh air.

He got hot under the collar.
She thought it was cool.
He gripped "ought" fiercely.
She thought "ought" was out of place.

He felt himself being moved out of his place.
He tried to get back into his place.
He felt himself becoming an Interloper.

<u>Warming</u>

"It's raining in the cloud," I write.

No matter how bright the moon,
how cloudless the sky,
it's tricky to write in the dark on scraps of paper
with the stub of a pencil
and be able to read what you've just written.

Just impressions
thought into words
impressed onto something flat and blank gleaned
from the trash.
Am I confident
that the inscription will match my thoughts,
that my thoughts will mean anything to me later,
when I tuck this shard of mental pottery
into the seventh archeological layer of the shoebox
under my bed?

Tonight there is a cloud
in the process of eclipsing the moon.
Good to have a cloud,
especially one of the tall fluffy ones.
They have been rare.

It's not raining here,
on the ground.

It's too hot.
The water vapor can form droplets
higher up in the air
but the droplets can't merge into bigger drops
with sufficient mass
to attract the attention of gravity.

It should be snowing up here in The Hills.
It's November.
But it's hot.

When I get up and
go outside into the dark,
early morning, 200AM,
the coolest part of the day,
I walk barefoot across the sparse dry grass,
tufts in parched dirt.
Everything out here smells like dry dirt.

I write,
"The moonlight on dusty brown mat fades."

We are in the florid stage
of this global dis-ease.
This part of the earth
is no longer covered with flowers.
Being red in the face,
if you've been outside
even for a little while in the day,
is no longer remarkable.
Even sexual fervor is burned out.
Can I still write beautiful verbally complex sentences?

I write, "I keep my hair cut short."

Is it cold outside?
Anywhere?

I lie down and close my eyes and feel the heat
penetrating my body.

There is no space left for writing.

Bones

They have taken the bones out of part of me
and put in new ones.

The new ones don't fit quite right.
The muscles don't wrap around them properly.
The tendons and ligaments don't attach in the right
places.
My movements have become awkward, clumsy.

I can feel the new bones
even when I am sitting very still, not moving.
They are there
inside of me,
part of me but not me.

I didn't ask for any of this.
I was chosen.

My right arm comforts me.
"I am still here."
"I am you."

They don't even knock
when they come now.

It's funny how their anesthesia only numbs the part
of me they are working on.
It's like they want me to be aware of what is being
done to my foot.

I looked it up:
The human foot is a strong and complex mechanical
structure containing 26 bones,
33 joints (20 of which are actively articulated), and
more than a hundred muscles, tendons, and ligaments.

I can tell that they didn't reconnect everything.

I don't try to run anymore.
I would just stumble and fall.
I would extend my good right arm to break my fall,
but I would just break my good right arm.
There really isn't any getting away.
They are going to do what they are going to do.

There is a gun with one bullet.
It is in the drawer of the table beside the chair where
I sit.
I try to be very still.
The gun with one bullet is in the drawer of the table
next to the arm of the chair
where my good right arm rests.

They left it for me when they took my left femur
and put in a new one.
I looked it up:
Your thigh bone (femur) is the longest and strongest
bone in your body.
Because the femur is so strong, it usually takes a lot of
force to break it.
The ball of the new bone doesn't fit well in the socket
of my hip.
It's actually a little too small.
My other new bones have been too big.

But the gun fits perfectly in my right hand,
as if it was custom made for me.
They want me to know that they understand detail
and accuracy
and can apply it when they want.

They don't knock when they come again.
I say, "Hello."

There is no reply, just movement.
I take the gun with one bullet from the drawer
and shoot one of them right between the eyes.
They are not deterred, not even a little.

They take my jawbone.
I looked it up:
The mandible, lower jaw or jawbone is the largest, strongest
and lowest bone in the human face.
It forms the lower jaw and holds the lower teeth in place.

They don't give me new teeth.
I can't say, "Goodbye."
But they leave my good right arm alone.
They give me a new bullet.

(Composed for Edgar Allen Poe Festival, Joslyn Castle, 2018)

David H. Reinarz

Fire

You allowed the fire to be set
Admit it
The match was lit
You could have grabbed the hand that held the match
My hand
You could have blown it out

You were swept up
The fire ate up all the oxygen in the room
You couldn't breathe
You rationalized that it enhanced your experience

It was a large, violent wildfire

You weren't merely willing to possibly get burned
a little
You bathed in it, wallowed, really, in the lake of fire

The fire created its own wind
The intense heat threw off vortices
The fire whirled
The fire torched husbands and ex-wives and kids
and friends, even a stranger or two
Did you know what would happen?
Did you care?

When I was done with you
I blew it out
Chilling, eh?

What was lost in the fire?
Nothing I cared about.
You?

David H. Reinarz

Beauty

The soft pink rose
climbing the wall of the old stone house
is rooted in cracked asphalt.

David H. Reinarz

Hands: Three Riffs

His Hands

She couldn't see what he was doing with his hands.
They were in a restaurant for God's sake.
A nice restaurant with white tablecloths and cloth
napkins.

The boy didn't have his hands in his pockets.
She could tell.
She knew what that looked like.
Arms by his side. Slouched in his chair. Sulking.
No.
His hands were in his lap and his breathing was a little
irregular.

She kicked her husband in the shins.
He lowered his newspaper in response.
She gave him the look that said, "do something about
the kid."
He gave her the "leave the kid alone " look
and went back to reading the sports page.
Who reads a newspaper in a restaurant with your
family sitting there?
What did she expect?
The Red Sox were in the playoffs..

She kicked the kid in the shins.
He glanced at her,
gave her the look that said, "Whaaat?!"

She gave him the look that said, "What are you
doing?"
Then she intensified her glare,
escalating her look to mean, "Show me your hands
right now, mister!"

The kid gave her the look that said, "Be careful what you ask for!"

She backed off.
Do ten year old boys play with themselves?
She shuddered. Of course they do.
Would a ten year old boy play with himself in a restaurant
with white tablecloths and cloth napkins?
She didn't know, and that really worried her.

The kid looked up.
She followed his line of sight across the room.
There was a girl, about the same age as her son.
Cute. No, pretty. Really pretty.
She was looking back at him.
She also had her hands in her lap.
Christ Almighty!

The girl was giving the kid the look that said, "You're way out of your league, buster."
The kid was giving the girl the look that said, "Oh yeah? You haven't seen me hit."
The girl giggled.

Maybe they were doing something innocent, she hoped,
like texting. Kids were always texting.
But the way they were acting, it might be that thing...that thing ...SEXTING.
Her heart rate red lined.

She kicked the kid again.
He gave her the "Whaaat?" look again.
She gave him the "I brought you into this world, and I can take you out!" look.

The kid gave her the look that said, "Governments can only govern with the consent of the governed, and I withdraw my consent as of this moment."
Just then the waiter arrived.

He had the birthday cake.
Her birthday cake.
She looked at the waiter.
She looked at the lonely sputtering candle.
A single tear leaked out of her left eye.
She was lonely and sputtering.
She gave the waiter the look that said, "What's a person to do?"
The waiter gave her the look that said, "Not my circus, not my monkeys."

Happily, the Red Sox had routed the Yankees in last night's game.
Happily, the kid was making progress in his quest for attention.
She dabbed at her eyes.
Happily, it would not be her job to wash the mascara out of the nice restaurant's white cloth napkins.

His Own Hand
He saw his own hand
His left hand
Sweep through his field of vision
His arm an uncontrolled vector
Cutting an arc
Through the space out from him and above him
His eyes tracking his own left hand
Like a rocket that had veered dangerously off course
after launching from Cape Canaveral.

It was then that he realized

That the exclamation "Oh shit!"
Was not being voiced by the scientists in the NASA
control room in Florida
But was issuing from his own mouth
As he felt his feet lose their grip on the stairs and
shoot out from under him.

There was an explosion of light
and stars filled the firmament of his unconsciousness
As his head bounced
Down
Down
Down
Until his body splashed
Onto the second floor landing.

Hand
He had the key in his hand,
his right hand,
as he drove through the city
to her house,
his left hand on the steering wheel.
He had the key
that she had given him just that day.

As he drove, he tapped the key on the rim of the
steering wheel.
Thinking of her.
Feeling all the feelings that she, by some magic, had
birthed in him.

He had met her a few months ago at an art exhibition
opening reception at one of his favorite galleries. He had
liked her immediately, the way she seemed fully engaged yet

aloof all at the same time as she passed through the gaggle of artsy patrons. Mysterious and attractive. They found themselves staring at the same photograph, each with a glass of grocery store grade pinot grigio in hand. They chatted about the seductive obsolescence of black and white shot on physical film and processed with noxious chemicals in a Parisian artist's garret. Maybe she was the one. He became aware of thinking this as he handed her his business card. She had smiled and then somehow vanished into the crowd.

> He turned into the driveway
> of her house
> and parked the car.
> Key in hand, he got out
> and walked up the sidewalk.

Although they had been dating regularly for several months, he hadn't seen her for over a week. She hadn't responded to phone calls or texts. She should have done. Then the key appeared.

The key had been a surprise. He liked surprises. It was delivered to his office by bicycle messenger. Inside the padded pouch was the freshly cut key with a note on which was an address and "Why don't you come over after work? I'm cooking."

> The door was already open.
> He entered.
> The heady aroma of sautéed onions and mushrooms
> filled the kitchen.
> She was standing at the stove,
> Stirring.
> In some 60's hippie girl peasant dress.
> Barefooted.
> Seductively obsolescent.
> He wrapped his arms around her waist.

She leaned back into his embrace.
He lifted up her skirt
and knelt to kiss her.
Her hips were naked in readiness.
There he found a bruise on the outside of her left
buttock.
He touched it.
She flinched slightly,
but didn't otherwise move.
He placed his hand
there.
The shape and size of the bruise mimicked his hand,
only larger.
Someone else had been there.
He withdrew.
He lowered her skirt
and gently smoothed out the wrinkles.

He quietly showed himself out.
He still had the key in his right hand.
He dropped it into the cup holder in the console,
started the car,
and shifted into reverse.
As he drove silently away, he noticed
peripherally
that her door
was still standing open.

Bukowski Goes to WalMart

The woman checking me out
at the discount chain store told me the total.
I handed her a wad of crumpled up bills and some
loose change.
It was the exact amount.
She looked at it.
She looked at me.
She counted it.
Twice.
"Have a nice day," she said.

I thought there was something in the quality of her
voice,
a tone.
Or maybe I was looking for a hint of judgement.
"Have a nice day. Really?" I replied evenly.
"Like, maybe I was having a not so nice day,
and you needed to recommend
an attitude adjustment?
Does my breath smell bad?
Does my scruffy unshaven face suggest despair?
Does my unkempt thrift store wardrobe hint at a life
in shambles?"

She just looked at me.
Completely non-plussed.
Like she gets this kind of rant from people all the
time.

"Thanks," I said, escalating.
"I WILL have a nice day.
I was going to go home
and close myself up
in the tiny dark coat closet

in my tiny dark bachelor apartment
and drink this bottle of cheap vodka
I just bought
until I passed out.
But now I won't,
because YOU told me to have a nice day.

Instead,
I'm leaving here
and I'm going to the Humane Society,
and I'm going to adopt an abused and abandoned
dog,
and I'm going to take him to the park
and play Frisbee with him
until we're both so tired that we want to puke.
And then the dog and I
are going to my tiny dark bachelor apartment,
and we are going to order in pizza,
and we are going to eat it on the floor together,
and we are going to watch TV
until we fall asleep in each others' arms.
And I will dream of me and my ex-girlfriend,
Hillary,
laughing and playing Frisbee in the park that one day
until we were so tired that we wanted to puke.
And in the morning,
when I wake up in a pile of pizza bones
and a puddle of dog pee,
and my pee,
I will remember that Hillary left me
for the Highway Patrol cop who wrote her a speeding
ticket
that day six months ago
when she slammed the door on her way out
of our tiny bright sunshiny couple's apartment.
And then I will take the dog back to the Humane
Society,

because I can't really take care of a dog properly,
or a girlfriend properly,
or even myself properly.
And then I will come back to this God forsaken
WalMart,
and I will buy TWO bottles of cheap vodka,
and, as you are checking me out,
I will tell YOU to have a nice day,
because SOMEBODY ought to have a nice day,
and I obviously don't know how to have a nice day.
I know how to sit alone in a tiny dark closet
in a tiny dark bachelor apartment
with two bottles of cheap vodka
and fantasize about lost love."

She didn't flinch.
She just looked me straight in the eye,
handed my the receipt,
and firmly replied,
"See you tomorrow, then, loverboy."

David H. Reinarz

How long

How long can you wait,
If you don't know the person is coming?

How long can you wait,
If you don't have an appointment?

How long can you wait,
If you don't know who it is you are waiting for?

How long can you wait,
If you don't even know why you are waiting?

You have to wait.
You have to wait, because
Whomever you are waiting for is not here yet,
Whatever will happen has not happened yet.

Even if you get up and walk away,
You will still be waiting,
So you sit there and drink another cup of coffee.
You don't read the newspaper.
You don't fall asleep.
You wait.

Then she walks in.
She doesn't walk by or past or over.
She walks in.
She laughs.
She was sitting at another cafe.
Drinking coffee, reading the news,
she even fell asleep.
She got tired of waiting.
She got up and walked away.
Then. Walked in. Here.

David H. Reinarz

<u>They Might Be Poems</u>

Every day since July of 2013, I have written a love poem for Lynne. I present it to her as we go to bed for the night. There are now over 2500 of them.

Some of them are pretty poetic and some are less like poems and more like journal entries or miscellaneous ramblings, but they might be poems, if you were feeling romantic at the moment you read them.

Here is her favorite:

A rivulet of sweat
meanders down your neck.

My lips follow.

ABOUT THE AUTHOR

David H. Reinarz is a writer of short stories and poetry. He is an alumnus of the 7 Doctors Writing Project in Omaha NE.

In 2015, he retired from a long career managing professional retail bicycle shops.

Dave and Lynne live in Omaha.